W9-AKE-041

Little Rabbit's
Easter Surprise

For John, with our love

Text copyright © 1992 by Joanne Compton
Illustrations copyright © 1992 by Kenn Compton
PRINTED IN THE UNITED STATES OF AMERICA
FIRST EDITION

Library of Congress Cataloging-in-Publication Data
Compton, Kenn.
Little Rabbit's Easter surprise / Kenn and Joanne Compton.
p.   cm.
Summary: Little Rabbit wants to help his father, the Easter Bunny,
decorate and distribute eggs for the holiday, but decides to keep
the one he has made for someone very special.
ISBN 0-8234-0920-1
[1. Easter—Fiction.   2. Rabbits—Fiction.]   I. Compton, Joanne.
II. Title.
PZ7.C7364Li   1992   91–17957   CIP   AC
[E]—dc20

Little Rabbit's Easter Surprise

Kenn and Joanne Compton

Holiday House / New York

CRASH!